Really, RAPUNZEL NEEDED A HAIRCUT!

The story of
RAPUNZEL
as told by
DAME GOTHEL

written by
Jessica Gunderson

illustrated by
Denis Alonso

Raintree is an imprint of Capstone Global Library Limited, a company incorporated
in England and Wales having its registered office at 7 Pilgrim Street, London, EC4V
6LB – Registered company number: 6695582

www.raintreepublishers.co.uk
myorders@raintreepublishers.co.uk

Text © Capstone Global Library Limited 2014
First published by Picture Window Books in 2014
First published in the United Kingdom in paperback in 2014

Edited by Jill Kalz, Catherine Veitch and Clare Lewis
Designed by Lori Bye
Art Direction by Nathan Gassman
Original illustrations © Picture Window Books 2014
Production by Victoria Fitzgerald
Originated by Capstone Global Library 2014
Printed and bound in China

ISBN 978 1 406 27985 6
18 17 16 15 14
10 9 8 7 6 5 4 3 2 1

British Library Cataloguing in Publication Data
A full catalogue record for this book is available from the British Library.

Let me tell you, it's lonely being a witch. When people find out what I am, they steer clear. I have no friends at all. Not one. It's unfair, really.

A sweet girl with beautiful hair once lived with me. And I used to have a fantastic garden. (Neither the girl nor the plants cared that I was a witch!) My flowers bloomed bright and tall. My radishes were to die for. But, sadly, I haven't seen the girl or my garden in a while. It all started when a neighbour tried to *steal* my radishes...

Here's how it went:

"My wife is going to have a baby," my neighbour stammered.
"And she craves your radishes. She swears if she doesn't
get them, she'll just die!"

"OK," I said. "But what will you give me in return? I can get a pretty penny for these at the farmers' market, you know."

"But I have no money. Not a single penny!" he whined. "Maybe I'll give you our baby? We can always have more, I guess."

Of course I agreed. A baby would be better than gold! It would cure my loneliness!

When the time came, the man brought baby Rapunzel to me. I raised Rapunzel as my own daughter and gave her anything she wanted from my garden: turnips, potatoes, berries, cucumbers ... But do you know what her favourite food was?

Radishes.

The girl had good taste.

All those vegetables helped Rapunzel's hair grow long and red. She sang sweet songs as she helped me tend the garden.

The longer Rapunzel's hair grew, the more she loved it. She washed it and combed it and brushed it and plaited it. And then she washed it again. You have no idea how much I spent on shampoo!

One day a group of neighbours gathered outside my garden. I heard them whispering. Plotting. Planning. This time, however, no one wanted to steal my radishes. They wanted to steal *Rapunzel* and use her hair for wigs!

Radish

So I did what any mother would do.
I locked Rapunzel away in a tower.

"Rapunzel, let down your hair!"

I would call. And she would lean out of the window and wrap her hair around a hook. Then I'd climb up.

Every day without fail, I brought her vegetables from the garden. At first she seemed content. But one day she told me she was lonely. And if anyone knows how loneliness feels, it's me. "How can I help?" I asked.

"Bring me every mirror you can find," Rapunzel said.

"Then I can keep myself company."

Pulling a load of mirrors to the tower wasn't my idea of fun, but I did it anyway. I spent a week gathering every mirror in the village. Then I lugged them, one by one, into the tower. Let me tell you, it was not an easy task for an old witch like me.

"Thanks!" Rapunzel said. "But I don't need the mirrors anymore. I met a handsome prince. He climbs up to visit me every day."

15

"What?" I roared, my voice rattling the windows and shattering the mirrors.

"He's going to steal you away!"

I panicked. What could I do? How could I keep the prince away? In a rage, I grabbed Rapunzel's hair and chopped it off. Clumps of it.

Rapunzel wailed. I admit I felt a little bad. "It'll grow back," I comforted.

"Short hair will be nice for the summer. Cooler."

But she would not stop crying.

17

"Let's go home, dear," I said. "I'll make you a radish salad, OK?" I fastened her hair clippings to the hook, and we crawled down together.

While Rapunzel ate her salad, I returned to the tower and waited.

"Rapunzel! Let down your hair!"
the prince called.

I lowered Rapunzel's
hair, and the prince
climbed up.

19

When the prince saw me, his eyes widened. I gave him my most evil cackle.

I'd meant only to scare him a little, but he leapt from the window and landed on some thorny bushes below. The poor boy staggered about, clutching his eyes. I was going to climb down and help him, but he did a terrible thing. He reached for Rapunzel's hair and yanked it from the hook. Then he ran away.

Since then I've been trapped in this tower. I try to sing sweetly in hopes of rescue, but my voice is sour. I try to grow my hair long, but my split-ends keep breaking off. Curse those mirrors for bringing me bad luck!

A little bird told me Rapunzel and her prince got married. I'm sorry I missed the wedding. It sounded lovely. Do you know what the bride carried? A bouquet of radish roses!

Think about it

Read a classic version of Rapunzel. Now look at the witch's version of the story. List some things that happened in the classic version that did not happen in the witch's version. Then list some things that happened in the witch's version that did not happen in the classic. How are the two stories different?

Most versions of Rapunzel tend to be told from an invisible narrator's point of view. This version is from the witch's point of view. Which point of view do you think is more honest? Why?

If you could be one of the main characters in this version of Rapunzel, who would you be, and why? Rapunzel? The prince?

How would other fairy tales change if they were told from another point of view? For example, how would Jack and the Beanstalk change if the giant was the narrator? What if the wolf in Little Red Riding Hood told that story? Write your own version of a classic fairy tale from a new point of view.

Glossary

character person, animal or creature in a story
narrator person who tells a story
point of view way of looking at something
version account of something from a certain point of view

Books in this series

978 1 406 27983 2

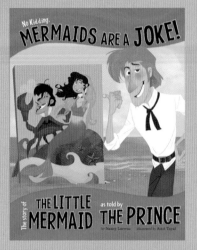

978 1 406 27984 9

978 1 406 27985 6

978 1 406 27986 3